Posing for Rodin

(and other random thoughts)
C.S. McGrail

Fintan and Turtle
Syracuse, New York U.S.A.

Posing for Rodin
© 2025 Fintan and Turtle
ISBN 978-1-944360-02-3

The book is a revised edition.

Please visit
http://www.fintanandturtle.com for other fine works of fiction.

To Melody Jane

Contents

Something Worth Shopping for

No one talks about it now,
but he was married once before,
years ago,
to a Turkish girl.

He was working over there when he met
her.
They dated for six weeks,
honeymooned for two,
then he was arrested for stabbing her
fifteen times.

His parents said it was self-defense.
Why else would he throw her corpse in a
dumpster?
They sold their house to cover his legal
costs.
But all to no avail.

He got eight years hard time, on foreign
soil, before coming home to a hero's
welcome.

I manage the apartments his parents live in.
They never did get their house back.
They don't know I know all this.
They think I'm too young;
as young as their son's new fiancée.
But they like me.
I'm polite.
Last week I got an invitation to the wedding.
I'm still undecided about what to get them.

I was thinking maybe steak knives.

That Would Hurt

The three-year-old is reaching through the
crib bars
trying to grab at the baby's face.

"What are you doing?" I ask.

"I want to touch the baby's eye."

"What? No. You can't. Why would you want
to do that?"

"To see what it feels like."

"Honey, if you want to know what an
eyeball feels like,
you should touch your own; not the baby's."

"No…that would hurt."

Adventures of an Unkempt Man

I was running errands a few Saturdays
back.
My hair looked like Medusa's.
So did my beard.
And I was wearing yesterday's clothes.

At one point, I was standing in line at the
Credit Union.
From behind me, a young voice yelled,
"There's Santa!"

I turned. A three-year-old boy was pointing
at me.
So much for cutting back on carbs.
I pointed back at him and said, "Hey Buddy,
how you doing?"

He immediately abandoned his family and
walked right over.

He stood so close; he had to look straight
up to see me.
I looked back down and said 'hi'.
He opened his arms like he wanted to get
picked up.
I looked over at his parents.

They were both terrified. Certain I was
homeless.
And flea infested.

I squatted down onto one knee and gave
the little guy a hug.
Hey, he could always ride home in the
trunk.

"Glad I got to see you, little man." I mussed
his hair. "But I can't stay."
He said, "I know." And put his hand on my
sleeve.

His father walked over to get him. I was
sure he was holding his breath.

I waved good-bye and stepped back in line.

When I finished at the counter, I looked for
him.
But the whole family had gone.
As I drove home, I passed a veterinarian's
office.
It made me wonder if you need an
appointment for rabies shots.

Posing for Rodin

I hope when I die, they call me a rebel,
a rascal, a rambler,
an outlaw or worse.
Let the truth of my tale be kidnapped and
slaughtered
then trampled and scattered and join me in
dust.

For what is the worth of a life gone
unnoticed,
slumped at the bar,
posed for Rodin?
Can we call him a man, with no legend to
linger?
No silver lined lies 'round the gray clouds of
life?

I spent my existence lying in waiting,
poised for the moment, jigger in hand;

Sat through the hours in smoldered
reflection,
scorched as the wings of Daedalus's son.
But the waiting was weighted, holding me
down,
till all that I could be, in days yet to come,
lay crippled, contractured, in comatose
song.

So sing the souls that sit here beside me,
a chorus of silence, the caste of the
damned.
Weren't we once the children, all wide eyed
and cuddly
with dreams of adventure to venture
beyond?
Weren't we once the pride, the hope of the
future;
the golden-haired chance to clasp the brass
ring?

How is it now, we've fallen as fodder,
struck down in battle 'fore battles begun?
How is it now so suddenly over,
so seemingly senseless to gasp our last
breath?

I hope when I die, they call me a rebel,
a rascal, a rambler, an outlaw or worse.
Don't waste your tears or flowers or
candles;
don't ask of your God in long ancient verse.
Just bid me farewell,
then forget that you knew me,
walk down the alley and piss where I slept.

Never look back, or the memories haunt
you and leave you forlorn as you face the
last call.

Grumblings

I'm always stuck with muffin butts for
breakfast.

The kids eat all the crispy, crunchy heads
and leave the rest.

They don't give a do-wha dang
that dad's the one that bought them,
or might enjoy an un-licked pastry for
himself.

I suppose I was the same when I was
younger,
a self-consumed munch mouth of a child.
Did my father always settle
for cherub fondled remnants,
of meals he might have otherwise enjoyed?

I remember we never ate his ice cream;
mad as spit when his

the only choice that could be had.

Who the hell eats Raisin Rum or Butter
Brickell?

I don't think the flavor even mattered;
it was just untouched by all but dear old
dad.

Running Backwards Thru Time

There wasn't much to choose from on
television.
After a bit of flicking, I found a quasi-
science show.
I say 'quasi-science' because they had
bleached all the math
and hard science out of it.
Even mudheads like me could follow along.

The narrator was talking about string
theory.
He said it was a part of Physics.
Scientists, he explained,
were looking for the smallest particles in the
universe.
So small, they weren't even three
dimensional.
Modern science offered equations that
pointed to this, they said.

These equations told anyone that knew
how to read them,
that these teeny, tiny, little things only had
length.
No width.
And no depth.
They were one-dimensional.
And, for whatever reason,
scientists christened these little buggers
'Strings'.

Strings, the narrator continued, would rattle
and shake
and somehow become quarks and protons
and neutrons.
But I had already stopped listening by then.
I couldn't wrap my head around the whole
'one-dimensional objects' idea.
How could such a thing be real?
Even reflections and rainbows were at least
two-dimensional.

I had to think about that.

I thought about it through the rest of that
science show.
Then I thought about it through three more
hours of late-night movies.
Then I got a scratch pad and a pen
and tried to think up my own one-
dimensional equations.
That gave me a headache.

I put down the pad
and tried not to think about it anymore.
But I found myself thinking about it again
when I was getting ready for bed.
And then at breakfast the next day.

I even thought about it at work,
where they were paying me to think about
something else.
Something they wanted me to think about.

I just couldn't picture a one-dimensional
object.
I was starting to think it was all just made-
up nonsense.

These things couldn't possibly be real.
 Maybe all those equations were just
gibberish.
And pretend.
Like the Emperor's new clothes.

Then I had an epiphany.
Thoughts.
Thoughts themselves are one-dimensional
objects.
They have length.
But no width.
And no depth.
And thoughts are real.
At least, I think thoughts are real.

Could the entire universe be made up
of millions of billions of trillions of teeny, tiny
little thoughts
just wiggling about?
Didn't seem likely.
But I couldn't come up with any other
examples of one-dimensional objects.

Now to be fair,
there could be an entire shopper's network
of one-dimensional objects out there.
I don't know.
Equation reading scientists might get to
pick and choose
to their heart's delight.
But I don't have that option.
Thoughts are the only one-dimensional
objects I get to work with.

So, I asked myself,
If the whole universe is made up of millions
of billions
of trillions
of these teeny, tiny little thoughts…

 Who's thoughts are they?

Someday

She used to live up on the Rez.
That's where she learned
to call the fire department "cellar savers".
It seems promptness was an issue.

She lived in that old house,
behind the dump, with her old man, Raw
Bones.
Raw Bones was a drinker.
He used to go up the street and get his ass
kicked,
then come home and still want to fight.

My wife knew her.
She knew everybody there and all of their
secrets.
My wife was the nurse at the free clinic.
She heard all the lies and saw all the truth.

And every story was always the same;
just some poor somebody, waiting on
someday.

One night, my wife got a phone call.
Seems that old house behind the dump
burned down.

The cellar savers, true to form,
assured that nothing would survive.
No trunks, or rug, or photographs,
No upholstery soaked in piss.
No ties that bind
or one more chance.…

Someday had arrived.

Let's

(Song for Melody)

Let's let our hair grow gray together.
Let's count the years rolling by.
Let's plant a tree
on the day that we're wed,
so our grandkids can swing from a tire.

Let's learn to walk with an uncertain
wobble.
Let's learn to sing like old crows.
Let's learn to make wine,
then hide a few bottles,
for someone to find when we're gone.

Let's always have breakfast for dinner and
lunch and cookies and pie when we wake.
Let's try not to worry,
and try not to cry.
Let's learn how to laugh at ourselves.

Let's sit in the park
or simply hold hands.
Let's do anything that you chose.

For all that I hope for
and all that I want
is to do all these things with you.

Things My Father Meant

Things my father meant to tell me
were lost in hesitation,
a frown,
a shrug,
then nothing more.
And all the things he knew,
he only said in silence,
until at last
there was nothing left to say.

No tales were told of army corps
or marriage on the rocks.
No hopes
or dreams
or bits of reason why.
And all the things he must have thought
laid shallow in a field,
swallowed by the low land fog of doubt.

Sometimes I watch my shadow when I'm
laughing,
I see an opaque man who never makes a
sound.

And it's sad to think
of all the things I've learned how not to tell
you,
and all the things I've meant to tell my
young.

One-ah Them-There Translator Apps

Some of my grandchildren started out as
twang talking hillbillies.
As they've become young adults, that has
receded quite a bit.
But when they were very small, it was
impossible to understand them.
Sometimes,
they couldn't even understand each other.

Once,
when the oldest of them was just 7, I was
babysitting him.
After an hour, a little friend of his got
dropped off.
His friend's mom was in a jam
and my daughter said I wouldn't mind,
so he came over for a few hours.

That was all fine,
but until that afternoon,
his little buddy had never met me before.

They were playing with trucks on the rug.
I was in the same room,
watching TV.

After a little while, the friend points at me
and says,
"Hooz they-et?"

My grandson answers,
"Ma momma's day-ed."

His little friend squinches up his face, all
confused, and says,
"Yo momma ain't day-ed. She zat work."

Somewhere South of Should Be

Once upon a time we went
and Oh! What a time it was
for wenting West of where we were
to Somewhere South of Should Be.

No map could tell us where to go
(for maps can't speak at all)
So each man made a pax as one
to plan, to plot, to path, to dance,
 to draw a passage back.
A course that ran from there to here,
that once reflected in a mirror,
would in reverse traverse reveal
Somewhere South of Should Be.

"First North, then fast, then East, then far."
In ink the route was wrote,
in amber hues
of blacks and two
we scribbled and described

a youthful place of open space,
a land of mine and yores,
where drinks get drunk
and thinks get thunk
and numbers never bind us.

"Tis mad!" says I
and "Aye!" says Tis.
(though between us agreement was rare)
We packed our lunch
and huffed a bunch and
set out towards the Sun.
On wheel, or wing, or foot, or hoof,
it mattered not the means we took
or if we saw, or conquered,
or made it home again.
For marching off as boys alone,
we knew we'd die as men.

Then all at once
disaster struck,
it shook us to the bone.
Tommy Smither's mom came out
and told him to come home.
"What kind of a woman end's a war before
it's even had?"
I threw my helmet in disgust
(which turned out to be mud)
and as I smeared the bigger chunks
in hopes to spare my hair,
I found out just what kind she was
to put the world on hold…

"I've got fresh baked cookies; tell all your
friends!"

And so it was that fateful day
when plans so grand were cast away
and honors great and soldier's pride
were quickly dropped and left outside.
Tomorrow bees a better day
for marching off to lands unknown,
for taking risks and living free,

lining up all duty's deeds,
for counting off in twos and threes
Somewhere South of Should Be.

Coyotes

Coyotes crowd a campfire
beneath a moonless sky
and fidget frozen fingers, as an oatmeal
cauldron simmers.

Beyond the dark a freighter shrills
like Banshee on the prowl.
And each man turns a crumpled collar,
clears his throat or stomps a foot,
then snuggles ever closer to the fading light
of life.

Seated still but sleepless,
one eye on old Jack Frost.
No wild and scruffy wolf dogs go howling till
the dawn.
Too old, too cold,
too full of wine,
too lost in mid-November.

The wind of was is on the air,
the carrion of change.

Slumber heads will dream tonight,
ice crystals on their lids until
one man more,
maybe two or three,
will miss the morning train.

Things I've Done

My wife's in the basement doing laundry.
I'm upstairs, in the kitchen.
There's a knock at the door.
It's the skinny kid from up the street
and she has a box of chocolates in her
hand.

"Your order come in."

I think she wants money but then she says
"Your wife already paid."

I thank her, take the candy and close the
door.
Then I yell down the stairs to my wife,
"Your order from the neighbor kid is here.
I'm opening it."

I'm about three pieces into it
and rummaging through the wrappers
when I hear…
BANG! BANG! BANG!
It's that same kid at the door again.

"I gave you the wrong order. You're
supposed to get this Calendar."

I stop chewing and look down at the box.

"Who gets these?"
"Mr. Breevey, across the street."
"He doesn't want a calendar?"
"He retired. He don't care what day it is."

I give her ten dollars and send her back to
Breevey's house.

"What do I say?"

"Tell him his order got canceled. Give him
the ten and the calendar."

After she leaves, I sit down and start back
in on the candy.
My wife comes up the stairs.

"I thought I ordered a calendar."

"No. That was Jack Breevey. Caramel?"

The Halloo Eternal

The western winds are calling me.
Not by name, or even with words,
But I know what they're saying.

Years ago, when I was a much younger
man,
I often confused recklessness for courage.

And when the winds would call, I would
chase them.
Much like an untrained dog suddenly off the
leash,
I would be gone for weeks.
Sometimes months.
Wandering without direction,
never sure where I was going.

I would sleep outside.
Under bridges. And in the woods.
I would eat in the orchards.

And drink from the rain.
It didn't matter that there was no
geographic destination.
I was certain that I would come home wiser;
knowing more than I did before.

But that was a fool's fantasy.
A delusion of the supine.
Whatever secrets the winds may hold,
they are not theirs to share.
They simply swirl past,
gathering up whatever is loose.

For the winds have no moral compass.
They know nothing of altruism.
Or compassion.
Or virtue.
Any good, or ill, that they may spawn
is of no concern to them.
Like nomads, they must wander.
Like Sirens, they must sing.
This is as it has always been.
And continues to deceive both derelict and
dreamer.

But I never understood any of that.
For years, I would come home,
time and again,
both broke and broken.
Family and friends were left frustrated and
confused.
They would whisper together in some other
room,

"What is wrong with him? What should we
do?"

But they already knew there was no
answer.
And rather than endure whatever nonsense
I might offer as retort,
their questions went unasked.
In appreciation of that silence,
I too said nothing.
And so it went. For a very long time.

I don't often think of those days anymore.
I speak of them even less.

There are now gardens to tend
and birds to feed.
And just sitting on the floor,
playing cards with a four-year-old,
reminds me, quite stiffly,
that I am no longer built
for sleeping on the ground.
Those days are gone.

But I also know,
that when I'm alone,
When everyone else is occupied,
And the Sun is setting and the clouds are
barely moving...

The Western winds are calling me.

The Festering Seeds of Worry

The night before the big event,
William Tell had a dream.
The soldiers marched his boy out 60 paces,
stood him in front of an oak tree
and placed an apple on his head.

Then they walked back to William
and in one swoop
chopped off both his hands.
One soldier gathered them up and
threw them in a pig trough.

William tried to sit up.
Someone else
would have to take the shot.
He couldn't see who it was.
He could barely see at all.

His boy stood tall,

not daring to move
or even glance around.
They both knew this was the end.

And as all went black,
William heard the pigs
fighting over his fingers.

School Days

I spent the entire 8th grade drawing big
asses,
and greasy moustaches
on all of my classmates and teachers.
Okay, not really on them.
In a notebook.
But I still drew them. And every day at
lunch,
my friend Carl Ackerman and I would go
through it.

We would make up stories about the
pictures.
Sometimes, we would string the stories
together,
like panels in a comic book.
That was our goal. To make comic books.
But mostly we made each other laugh.

We tried to make the other kids

at the lunch table laugh too.
One time, Carl laughed so hard at his own
story that he choked on his chocolate milk.
It sprayed out his nose.
Everyone laughed at that.

Everyone, except Carolyn Shaughnessy.
She sat across the table from Carl.
He gave her an 'Already-Been-Chewed'
make over.

She screamed. Then cried.
Then ran and told on us.
We got in trouble. I don't know why.
Okay, I do know why.
One of the teachers looked in my notebook.
Then two other teachers did too.
They saw themselves with big asses
and greasy moustaches.
They didn't like that very much.
One teacher said they were going to throw
my book
in the incinerator.
Do middle schools even have incinerators?

I didn't know. I was thirteen. I believed him.

And, oh yeah,
Carl and I couldn't sit together at lunch any
more.
That was the worst part.
I was mad for a while.
And I secretly hated Carolyn Shaughnessy.
I didn't tell anyone, but I changed her name
to Puke-us Mucus.
And mumbled it to myself every time I saw
her.
She didn't care.
She didn't even look at me.

But after about three weeks,
my notebook came back.
It showed up one morning, in my locker.
I guess the incinerator must have been
broken.

I don't know how it showed up.
It just did.
Okay, that's not quite true.

I do know how. I just didn't know who did it.
I tried to find out. But didn't get anywhere.
I even looked through the notebook, hoping
for a clue.
I kind of, sort of, found one. At least I
thought so at first.
But it was a dead end.

In the bottom corner of the very last page of
the notebook,
someone had drawn a big, round, hairy
bug.
At least I thought so.
Carl disagreed. He said it looked like
what you would get when you scribble,
to make a pen start working.
I thought it looked more on purpose than
that.
I wanted to ask a few people. But I decided
not to.
I didn't want anyone to find out I got my
book back.
I just left it in my locker and hoped
someone would break in again

and give me another clue.

See, anyone that wanted to, could get into
my locker.
That's how the book came back in the first
place.
The lock part of my locker, worked fine.
But there were no hinges on the other side.
Never were,
from what I could tell.
Whenever I opened the door,
it would come completely off the frame.
Anyone with a plastic ruler could pry it
open.

Every day,
I would lean the locker door against the
wall,
while I got out my books
or hung up my coat.
Sometimes Mr. Peyote, the art teacher
across the hall,
would stare at me.
His name wasn't really Mr. Peyote.

We just called him that because he was so
weird.
He would watch me, at my locker, but never
came over
or said anything.

Carl said Mr. Peyote was high all the time
and thought the whole thing was a
hallucination.
That's why he never said anything to me.
Carl also said I should wait until Peyote was
watching,
then climb into the locker and pull the door
back into place, behind me.
Just to mess with his head.
We both laughed at that. But I never did it.

There was one other teacher that came by,
one time,
and told me I had to get the locker fixed.
I didn't want to.
But before I could think up anything to say,
Terry Hillbach said, "It's already on Mr.
Mackey's list."

Terry had the locker next to mine.
Unlike me, he was a straight A student.
And after high school graduation, he went
on to one of the military academies.
His parents groomed to be a leader.
And he always spoke with confidence.
So, all the teachers believed everything he
said.
We all thought that was pretty funny.
Especially Terry.

See,
he didn't say that about my locker because
it was true.
He said it because he knew I wanted the
teacher to just go away.
So, he said it.
And it worked.
He was a good guy.

The Mr. Mackey he was talking about
was the school maintenance man.

You had to get on his 'fix-it' list to get
anything done.
Mr. Mackey was older than the mummy.
And smelled like a horse barn.

I didn't care that my locker was broken.
And I didn't care if it ever got fixed.
But if I had been forced to,
I would have had to go down in the
basement
and fill out a work ticket.
That wasn't ever going to happen.

See,
before we first came to middle school,
back at the end of 5th grade,
we did a field trip, and visited what would
become our new school.
Some of the 8th graders were told to give us
a tour.
They did.
And while they did, they told us terrible,
awful, scary stories
about Mr. Mackey,

a guy none of us had ever seen or met
before.

They said he lived down in the school
basement,
which was really a torture chamber
dungeon.
They said he ate lost children.
Sometimes three a day.
And that he had an evil face that grew out
of the middle of his chest.
And when he opened his shirt all the way,
the evil face would jump out and scream,
in some forgotten, devil language,
and it would hypnotize you.
It would make you a zombie slave with its
crazy, lightning bolt eyeballs.
And you would go down to the dungeon, in
a trance, to be eaten.
And being the naive, dim-witted, 10-year-
old that I was,
I believed every word.
I was scared shitless of Mr. Mackey.

But not Carl Ackerman.
Carl loved all those stories.
He thought Mr. Mackey was way cool.
He wasn't scared at all.
Every day, starting the first day of 6th grade,
Carl would go find Mr. Mackey
and talk to him.
Sometimes he talked so much he was late
for homeroom.
Which got him in trouble.
But Carl didn't care.
He thought homeroom was stupid.
Which it was.

Sometimes at lunch, when I didn't have
new pictures to talk about,
Carl would tell me what Mr. Mackey had
said.
But Carl would always turn everything into
an amazing adventure.
So, when he talked about Mr. Mackey,
I would draw crazy, apocalyptic pictures to
capture it.

Carl had so many stories about Mr. Mackey
that we started tying them together.
We even talked about making a movie out
of them.
We were going to call it "Swamp Mutant
Three".
I don't know why it was three.
It was our first movie. But that's what we
called it.

In the movie, Mr. Mackey survived a
radioactive waste disaster.
But he was mutilated and glowed
radioactive green all the time.
Everyone was afraid of him.
So, he ran away and hid in the swamp so
people would stop tormenting him.

Carl wanted him to be a good guy.
But a good guy that everyone was afraid of;
like the Hulk or the Thing.
Seemed to me, there was a bit of truth to
that part of the story.
But I was still terrified of our hero.

I wasn't in any hurry to find out, one way or another.

In the movie, Swamp Mutant only had one friend.
A kid named Carl.
But Swamp Mutant couldn't say 'Carl'
cause his face was all bashed in and burnt up.
So, he called him 'Nar-el'.

None of the other characters in the movie were smart enough to figure out that Carl and Nar-el were the same person.
They all had fat asses and greasy moustaches.
So, Carl could do all the daytime investigating
and report back to Swamp Mutant on what he uncovered.

It was going pretty good.
And I was starting to like the story.
Then my notebook got taken.

That changed everything.

Even after I got it back. It wasn't the same.
Carl and I weren't allowed to sit together at
lunch.
We didn't talk like we used to.
We were still pals. It was just different.
Then summer came.

And the next year was high school.
I was getting prepped for college.
And Carl joined Future Farmers of America.
They taught him blacksmithing.
And welding.
And small engine repair.
We didn't have any classes together.

At the time, all the college bound kids
thought that what Carl was doing was
'dumb kid' stuff.
Mostly because you had to get your hands
dirty.
But looking back,

those of us that thought that way were the
dumb ones.
Carl was smarter than the rest of us.

I still see him. He's trying to be retired.
We get together for lunch about once a
month.
He just sold one of his businesses.
And gave the other one to his grandsons.
But Carl can't sit still. He will be starting up
something new soon.

I still see Terry Hillbach too.
His granddaughter plays softball a few
blocks from my house.
In the summer, I walk over to watch them
play.
Terry is always there.

About my third year of college, Mr. Mackey
died.
I was home for the summer.
So, when Carl told me, I said I would go to
the funeral with him.

And I did.
But deep inside I was still afraid.
And I kept thinking about all those stories I
was told.
I didn't say anything to anyone, of course.
But I did shutter for no reason at the funeral
home.
I don't think anyone saw me.

Mr. Peyote was there too,
paying his respects.
He recognized me and nodded.
I was surprised.
I was taller and had a beard.
But he left right away. So we didn't get to
talk.
That was the last time I saw him.
Which was unfortunate.

See, that summer my parents sold their
house
so they could move south.
I wasn't going with them,
so I had to go through my stuff.

Whatever I didn't want,
or take back to school, was getting tossed.

That's when I found my old notebook.
It was on a shelf, in the back of my closet.
I almost threw it out. But then I opened it.
And flipped through it. It was fun.
Kind of sad, in a nostalgic sort of way.
But overall, fun to have.

I decided to keep it before I finished looking
through it.
And figured at some point I would
eventually show it to Carl.
Which I did,
twenty years later, when I moved back to
town.

We got together for dinner and drinks.
We were both married to girls we didn't
know back in 8th grade.
So, when I pulled out the notebook,
there were lots of stories to tell.

We all laughed for over two hours, looking
at the pictures
and listening to Carl.

And then at the very end,
Carl stopped in mid-sentence
and very slowly said
"Oh. My. God!"

We all looked.
He was pointing to the mysterious scribble
bug on the last page.
And it was then that I realized something
that I could have never possibly known way
back in 8th grade.
The big, round, hairy, scribble bug wasn't a
bug at all.
It was a peyote button.

Lessons in Liquidity

The cautious eye of doubt is upon me.
"The water's big and it goes down."

How true.
The water is big, much bigger than her,
and only too happy to disappear down that
tiny hole.

How do I explain the three states of matter
and why she and her sister,
but not the suds,
are safe inside the tub?

Flashes of cartoon cats
inside faucet drips
and coyotes, shaped like drain pipe traps
flicker behind my eyes.
And just for a moment I see the world as
she might.

It seems logic,
like most other intoxicants,
is merely an acquired taste.

I lift each one out and wrap them in their
towels.

Then I put the youngest on my knee.
We watch a whirlpool of water wiggle
and wag its way into non-existence.

"Hear that slurpy noise? I can make your
belly do that."
She squeals
and squirms her way loose,
running from the room
as I chase her on my knees.

Somewhere Along the Way

My parents always viewed it as an
obligation.
It was how they were raised and how they
raised us.
I really don't know, but was taught to
believe
that at one time, all of us were raised that
way.

Perhaps I was misinformed.

Some of my friends
and especially some of my friend's children
don't act like they were raised to be
thankful.
I often wonder what goes through their
heads when
they first get up or finally lay down each
day.

It's probably best that I don't know.

Sometimes, when I ponder the current state
of the world,
I wonder if there is some sort of intertwined
correlation there;
cause and effect, perhaps.
Some days I am absolutely sure of it.
But I can't prove anything so I don't say
anything.

But I can tell you this:

It is very difficult to stay angry,
or be self-indulgent,
or righteously indignant
when you remember to be thankful.
Somewhere along the way,
we should all stop; each one of us,
and think about that.

The Sound of One Hand Napping

What if the only two things that God can
say
are "Not just yet"
and "I already know that."
What if science is a just a circle jerk
and logic a shallow pool?
What if your IQ
is nothing more than a blister on your soul?

What if sanity's a passing phase
and poverty's a sin?
And time's a shadow,
a mere mirage
that doesn't exist at all?
What if desire gives you cancer
or laughter makes you age?
What if any chance for inner peace
is ruined because you speak?

What if personality is just a veil
hiding you from yourself?
What if "Inheriting the Earth" was a horrible
threat
instructing you not to be meek?
What if the Devil thinks you're easy
and Jesus thinks you're dumb?

Or the juice of life isn't worth the squeeze
and you still can't get it right?

What if heaven has an unpleasant smell
and people you don't like are there?
What if life is just preamble,
until your final day,
and it's the last four seconds that count for
all,
would you know what to think or say?

Beneath the Lighthouse

My father was a shipwrecked seaman, and
I his shipwrecked son.
He never learned to navigate; the knots he
tied were none.
Mama said he had no Pa and this I know as
true.
The old man drown, before his birth, so
Captain-less he grew.

But every tide he went to sea, to see what
sailors saw,
and after months of being gone, he'd wash
up on the shore.
We'd brush the sand and wring him out and
often wonder why
the other sailors came to port; their clothes
completely dry.

And so it was for years and years, an
endless pointless dream,

we'd sit in chairs and watch the sea
beneath the lighthouse's beam.
Then one day it's over…
they brought him home in chains and told
Mama,
"He's a lubber now. He won't go out again."

"He'd dine each day on cold sea broth with
nothing more to eat.
Then try to walk the ocean floor, with
anchors on his feet.
Charts and maps he'd steal at night and
feed them to the fish;
then swim a course of broken circles 'round
some sunken ships."

They left him in a soggy slump unchained
but not unbound
and there he spent his final days adrift on
solid ground.

I watched him as he watched the waves
and sang in garbled voice
a song of sailors lost at sea, with eyes all
glazed and moist.

That fall he died of lizard lump and Ma of
too much sleep.
My sister's married; has a child, and I the
light house keep.
The names of stars,
the names of knots,
I learn to pass the time,
then gaze each evening out to sea, and
have a cup of brine.

Reluctant Churchgoers

When young, our granddaughter was a very
restless child.
At 6, she had no time for sitting still.
Or reading. Or even watching TV.
She would much rather run around
or climb a tree.

The idea of taking her to church didn't strike
me as particularly plausible.
But that was the request from mom,
before she deployed overseas.

My wife and I are not regular church goers.
And our granddaughter, safe to say, had no
interest in
being a churchgoer of any kind.

But I had agreed, so we went.

To her credit, she did better than I
expected.
She mostly mumbled to her dolly. And
occasionally glared at me.
But overall did very well.

"That wasn't so bad." I said, as we reached
the car.
"Any part of church you happen to like?"
"Leaving." She grumbled.
Then, thinking she was in trouble,
turned towards the window, stern puss.

I was amused. We were still getting to know
one another.
After a pause, I said, "I don't know if it's my
favorite part, but I like leaving too."
She pretended she wasn't listening, but she
was.

I started the car. And let it idle.

"If you like leaving, why do you even go?"

Pretty sharp for 6, I thought.

"I don't mind going." I said, bending the
truth.
"But if I don't go, I can't leave. And if I can't
leave,
I don't get my after-Church waffles."

Breakfast was a head turner. Our eyes met
in the mirror.
"Unless you'd rather go back in?"
I pointed at the church.
"Granny's waiting." she said, locking herself
into her car seat.
I smiled. And put it the car into gear.

The Blood of Au

From whence he came I cannot say
nor how far back in time.
But from a cauldron, in a pit,
he crawled out with a grin
and knew full well, that all mankind
would claim him for their God.

And so he slashed his only limb
with a knife held in his teeth
and sprayed his spew upon the fields
that all of us would eat.
Unsuspecting, unrelenting, we ate a hearty
feast
and found ourselves with one desire;
to taste the Blood of Au.

It starts out sweet upon the lips
but bitters in the throat,
 then burns the brain like rabid plague
till women caste their young aside,

and men grow wicked with deceit
and boast of cunning lies.

While everyone blames everything
and no one gives a damn;
it grows and flows and spawns it's young
that they may do the same.
And all the world turns black and cold
in hellish pagan prayer,
to satisfy that one refrain;
that endless, quenchless need,
to rectify the hollow soul
and taste the Blood of Au.

So plant for him the burning bush
atop the mountain high
and tell yourself you hear his voice
within the amber flames
that crackle like a boisterous hag,
who glees at your demise.

For someday soon,
you'll take the plunge
and swim the other side,

then stand before the silent one
as naked as a babe.

And everything you've ever done,
or thought,
or want,
or said;
will grovel at his humble feet and offer no
defenses.

And will you stand so straight and tall
with eyes still sharp and focused
and state with pride or earnest zest
the life you led was wasted?

For every moment grace was offered,
for every choice not taken,
you never gave a second thought
but pushed your way before him
and hoped with all your heart and soul
that this event was endless
and you at last would reign supreme
and taste the Blood of Au.

Finding Value at the Mall

I'm sitting in the food court killing time.
A three-year-old walks up
and announces he has just burped in his
pants.

I smile
and confess that,
I too,
sometimes burp in my pants.

Then his mother shows up.
And offering no pants burping stories of her
own,
takes him away.

Now, if I had made my daughter and her
friend take the bus home,
like I threatened,
I would have missed that.

Smoke Signals

I try not to laugh
as I empty the can,
less the other two think
I like to watch things burn.
Who else but me
would think any of this is funny?
But it's so easy.

I got twenty-six hundred bucks
in parts and upholstery,
plus, half of eight grand
for stealing the thing.
I even thought about keeping it;
but that ain't the gig.

People still burn trash on the Rez
and they don't have a fire department worth
mentioning.
Everyone else stays out
unless invited, escorted or both.

Someday they'll make us pay a tax
to keep the outside law at bay,
but for now,
we're just another occurrence of illegible
smoke signals after dark.

The River

Like a native maiden's hair
the river's course run thick and black;
it's waters deep and still.
I sit on the banks
and watch her as she selflessly twists and
turns.
I love her
And I love being with her,
watching her,
riding her,
 sleeping next to her.

I can't imagine any other life.

What lies beyond the next bend?
How rough will it get?
How beautiful the sunset
or luminous the stars?
It doesn't even matter…

It's the river that holds my heart.
Being with her
is both the adventure
and the reward.
She holds all the secrets to life
and as I learn to listen,
they are revealed slowly,
deliberately,
with a gentle force that only truth holds.

I love the river.

The river is you.

Conversation with a 9-Year-Old

Can we go to McDonald's?

Not today, I don't have any money.

You have fifty dollars on your dresser.

Yes, I do.
But that's a tank of gas.
And six dollars in tolls, to take you back to
your mother's house.
Whatever is left, is coffee for the week at
work.
So, you're right.
I do have money.
I just don't have money for McDonald's.

Well, how about Burger King?

Fishing off the Island of Doubt

Somewhere; the water's calmer.
Somewhere; the water's clear.
Somewhere; the current runs consistent
and tides respect the clock.

Somewhere; lines never get tangled.
Somewhere; nets are never snagged.
Somewhere; anglers catch their fill
and go home satisfied.

Somewhere; fishing tales run true.
Somewhere; persistence pays.
Somewhere; all these things can happen,
but it's not here.

Another Poet's Dead

Another Poet's dead, and those I know to
weep are none.
Another time has come but those we call to
rise still slumber.
Another chance is lost and those that might
have gained just shrug.

An old man once said to me,
"I remember back, before I was born,
there was a Togo woman with a shark
toothed grin.
She sang, 'We have all been here before.'
You'd think we would have learned by
now."

And how many times have we seen it so?
How many circles round the Sun?

Another place to start again, and yet we
build it just the same.

Another face, to fill the space, but still our
goal is un-evolved.
Another phrase to quote or quoin but yet
our wit is just as trite.

That same old man just smiled and said,
"You'll remember once you're gone,
 a soldier born with snake eyed skin hums,
'Nothing really changes, that's why we're
always here.'
You'd think we would have learned by now.
You'd think we would have learned."

They're Not Opposites

He looked at me and shook his head
in frustrated disgust.
"You're about as smart as you're going to
get." He spat.
"Oh, you might learn a few parlor tricks,
or a bit of somewhat interesting trivia to
recite,
but as far as raw intelligence goes;
you're done."

I hung my head.

He watched me stand there
then felt bad for being so honest.
Putting a hand on my shoulder,
he continued, a little softer,

"I know. That's disturbing. But there is
hope."

I peered up at him.

"Since you're not going to get any smarter,
you might want to focus on being a whole
lot less stupid.
You see, contrary to popular belief,
they're not opposites.
They co-exist.
The smartest people in the world do dumb
shit all the time;
they get lost, or burn their fingers.
They forget what they were going to say
or they misplace things...
but they're really, really smart so nobody's
too concerned."

"You on the other hand;
you need to distance yourself
from stupid as much as possible."

I scratched my head; uncertain.

"Now that may sound tough
but it's really not all that hard.
It's called 'paying attention'.
Now go on, get out there and give it a try."

God of War

My oldest grandson is now 17.
We live 900 miles apart.

But we text almost every day.
Today he wrote, "Papa! I won!"

"Uh… Okay, cool?"

"Papa, it's that game I was telling you
about. I won God of War!"

"Oh yeah! Very cool. Congratulations!
So now you go to the next level?"

No, I won! I kicked ass on the whole thing!"

"Oh. Okay, very good. What are you going
to play next?"

"I don't know yet."

"I can't speak for her, but I bet your mom
would like it if you kicked ass on
God of Household Chores."

"Papa!"

"Or maybe God of Gainful After School
Employment."

"Those aren't games."

"How do you know? You've never played
them."

"I got to go."

"Ha-ha! I imagine you do. Talk more
tomorrow.
Love you."

"Love you too."

Remember to Wipe Your Feet

Where do you think thoughts come from?
That is,
if you're inclined to think such things of
thoughts.
Are they hatched in the hollows of your
humble hat holder?
Did they have a life before you think you
thought them up?
Do they die as abruptly as your attention
span,
or do they live on
half completed and handicapped,
hobbling around inside your head?

Can they drain out when you're asleep
or no one's home?
Can they slither into another as you
slumber,
causing that person to awake,
half baked,

thinking your thoughts are their own and
wonder,
'Where do you think thoughts come from?'

Do they ever get hungry
cooped up all day inside your skull
with nothing to do but bounce around
chasing echoes?
Is that why they invented books;
to feed a starving thought?
(maybe fatheads just read too much)

I know they must eat something
because I've seen some thoughts swell up
so huge,
and weigh a man down so heavy,
he can hardly stand erect.

Finds himself walking through life, all
shuffle foot
and hunched over
wondering how he got like that,
carrying the burden of all them thoughts;
worry and wishing they'd just go away.

But them thoughts never do,
they just keep making things heavier and
harder,
complaining out loud
of crowded quarters and cramped
conditions,
demanding more room to breed and
burrow,
snuggling in and pushing down.

And all the while
this fellow's slumping farther still,
sweating and swearing under the load,
short of breath,
tired and sleepless,
bug eyed bent
with the rusty taste of blood in every
swallow,
running faster,
jumping higher,
till finally falling flat…
pinned to the Earth in rigor mortise,

never to think again.

What happens to thoughts then?
Do they die too?
Do they sink into the soil and decay,
never to live again?

Or do they wash away like rain,
making puddles on the ground
or streams along the side of the road
running downhill
to a house full of new hosts to hide inside?

Would you know enough to look out for
them
as you run to your car
at the end of each day?
Would they ripple and splash
as you stomp through them,
soaking your shoes and the cuffs of your
pants?

Would they cling for dear life to the tips of
your trousers
hoping to hang on
till you bring them back home
so they can feed off the frenzy of the
coaxial cable?

Is that what they do? Is that how they
grow?
And what of the people you talk to and
love?
What of your family and friends and
neighbors and chums?
Are they suddenly thinking thoughts
they've never thought before, thoughts you
thought were yours?

Well, tell me dear friend,
when you came home today…

Did you remember to wipe your feet?

ACKNOWLEDGEMENT

The Cover Art to this work was created by photographer Melody J. Burnam.

www.ingramcontent.com/pod-product-compliance
Lightning Source LLC
Chambersburg PA
CBHW070446170726
48291CB00005B/1623